Everybody Has Something Slightly Askew

Sally Huss

ISBN: 10: 1-94574247X
ISBN 13: 9781945742477

Everybody has something slightly askew.

What about you? What's different with you?

There is a lady who has hair growing from
the bottom of her feet.
You might not think this is so neat,
But you should see what she can do with her hairy feet.

She can dance from dawn 'til dusk

And at the same time pick up the dust.

Everybody has something slightly askew.

What about you? What's different with you?

Have you heard about the man who has monkey bars

growing out of his ears?

You won't find him in tears.

Instead of hanging from his knees or his toes,

He's learned to hang from his nose!

Everybody has something slightly askew.

What about you? What's different with you?

Then there is the potter who had more arms

than he knew what to do with…

Until he set up some wheels to mold tons of clay with.

Now he can make a set of dishes in ten seconds flat

And with his other arms fix a meal. How about that?

Yummmm!

Everybody has something slightly askew.

What about you? What's different with you?

Having an extra set of eyes

Proved to be quite an asset for two special guys.

They were in an unusual circumstance for sure.

Being born conjoined twins, there was no cure.

Each wanted to go his separate way,

But their predicament forced them to stay.

To keep them going in one direction,

They needed to be under each other's inspection.

So these extra sets of peepers

Allow them to be their brother's keepers!

Everybody has something slightly askew.

What about you? What's different with you?

These are crazy examples, that's absolutely true.

But perhaps your "differentness" is something that is bothering you.

It may be being chubby, having pimples, freckles or red hair,

Or something you have to do or wear.

Some children must walk with the help of crutches or braces…

While others have braces in the oddest of places.

Some kids must get around in a wheelchair,

But they can still go almost anywhere.

Some children have trouble with their hearing,

But find a hearing aid helpful to be wearing.

Seeing is hard for some lads and lasses,

But their sight is corrected by wearing glasses.

Speech and language can certainly be difficult for some.

Even breathing for those with asthma

can be a challenge to overcome.

Then there are brave kids with diabetes,

Who vow that, "Nothing will ever defeat us."

They must watch their blood sugar to be

at the top of their game.

While kids with food allergies must pay attention

to their food to do the same.

Sometimes it is an allergy to peanuts, milk, eggs or fish,

Or something with soy or wheat in a dish.

Some with obvious differences can be bullied or teased.

Those that do it have a particular disease.

It could be called "a lack of kindness."

But no need to be bothered by them or be driven into shyness.

vanilla
cherry
toffee
peanut
Rocky
straw-
berry
Blueberry
Banana

chocolate
coffee
lemon

crunch
Road

Apple

Almond
Pistachio

Just like flavors of ice cream, if everyone were the same,

Life would be so very plain.

So enjoy your peculiarities, your differences, your specialness,

Just as you enjoy your sameness.

And remember, everybody has something slightly askew.

Not just you! Not just you!

The end,
but not the end
enjoying yourself
just as you are.

At the end of this book you will find a Certificate of Merit that may be issued to any child who has fulfilled the requirements stated in the Certificate. This fine Certificate will easily fit into a 5"x7" frame, and happily suit any girl or boy who receives it!

Sally writes new books all the time. If you would like to be alerted when one of her new books becomes available or when one of her e-books is offered FREE on Amazon, sign up on her website, www.sallyhuss.com.

If you liked *Everybody Has Something Slightly Askew,* please be kind enough to post a short review for it on Amazon. Thank you.

Here are a few Sally Huss books you might enjoy. They may be found on Amazon.

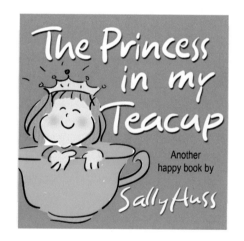

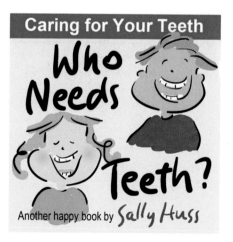

About the Author/Illustrator

Sally Huss

"Bright and happy," "light and whimsical" have been the catch phrases attached to the writings and art of Sally Huss for over 30 years. Sweet images dance across all of Sally's creations, whether in the form of children's books, paintings, wallpaper, ceramics, baby bibs, purses, clothing, or her King Features syndicated newspaper panel "Happy Musings."

Sally creates children's books to uplift the lives of children and hopes you will join her in this effort by helping spread her happy messages.

Sally is a graduate of USC with a degree in Fine Art and through the years has had 26 of her own licensed art galleries throughout the world.

This certificate may be cut out, framed, and presented to any child who has earned it.

Certificate of Merit

_____
(Name)

The child named above is awarded this
Certificate of Merit for:

*Being kind to others who may have disabilities
*Being grateful for what you have
*Being patient with others

Presented by: _____

Date: _____

Made in the USA
Lexington, KY
30 May 2019